THE WORLD OF ASTRID LINDGREN

MEET

PiPPi

LONGSTOCKING

OXFORD
UNIVERSITY PRESS

Great Clarendon Street, Oxford OX2 6DP
Oxford University Press is a department of the University of Oxford.
It furthers the University's objective of excellence in research, scholarship,
and education by publishing worldwide. Oxford is a registered trade mark of
Oxford University Press in the UK and in certain other countries

Pictures converted by Tom Heard
Translated by Elisabeth Kallik Dyssegaard,
used by agreement with Rabén & Sjögren Agency

First published in 1947 by Rabén & Sjögren, Sweden
as Känner Du Pippi Långstrump?

For more information about Astrid Lindgren, see www.astridlindgren.com.
All foreign rights are handled by The Astrid Lindgren Company, Lidingö, Sweden.
For more information, please contact info@astridlindgren.se.

First published 1947
This edition 2020

British Library Cataloguing in Publication Data

Data available

ISBN: 978-0-19-277242-8

1 3 5 7 9 10 8 6 4 2

Printed in China

Paper used in the production of this book is a natural,
recyclable product made from wood grown in sustainable forests.
The manufacturing process conforms to the environmental
regulations of the country of origin.

MEET PiPPi LONGSTOCKING

BY ASTRID LINDGREN

ILLUSTRATED BY
INGRID VANG NYMAN

OXFORD
UNIVERSITY PRESS

MEET THE CHARACTERS

Tommy

Annika

Pippi

Mr Nilsson

Pippi's horse

CHAPTER 1

Pippi Comes to Villekulla Cottage

Here are Tommy and Annika, two nice, well-mannered little children. They are playing croquet in their yard. It's okay.

'But I'd still like to have a friend,'
says Annika.

'So would I,' says Tommy.

Next to Tommy and Annika's yard
is another yard. In it is a house called
Villa Villekulla. No one lives there.
The house is empty.

'It's so silly that no one wants to

move into that house,' says Tommy.

'Yes,' says Annika.' Someone should live there. Someone with children.'

CHAPTER 2

Pippi at Home

One beautiful day when Tommy and Annika peer over the fence surrounding Villa Villekulla, they see something very strange.

A little girl is
walking across the
yard, carrying a
BIG horse.

Tommy and Annika can't believe their eyes, because a little girl can't lift a horse. But this girl can.

Her name is Pippi Longstocking,
and she is so incredibly strong that
there is not a policeman in the whole
world who is as strong as she is.

She is also rich. She has a big bag full of gold coins. And now she has moved into Villa Villekulla.

She's going to live there all alone with her horse and her little monkey, who is called Mr Nilsson. Pippi has no mum or dad, which is fine with her, because that means there's no one to tell her that she has to go to bed just when she's having the most fun. She always does exactly as she pleases.

'Do you want to have breakfast at my house?' Pippi asks Tommy and Annika.

'Yes, thank you,' they say.

'Who's cooking?' asks Annika.

'I am,' says Pippi.

Pippi does everything herself. Now she is making pancakes. When a pancake is done, she throws it way up in the air and over to Tommy and Annika, who are sitting on the firewood chest, stuffing themselves.

'Those were the best pancakes I've ever had,' says Tommy.

Pippi has a broken egg in her hair. It landed there when she was beating the pancake batter. But Pippi doesn't care.

'They say that egg yolks are good for your hair,' she says. 'Just wait, my hair will grow like crazy.'

Pippi also bakes cookies. She rolls out the dough on the kitchen floor.

'Because the counter just isn't big enough when you are baking at least five hundred cookies,' says Pippi.

Mr Nilsson, the little monkey, helps her. But the horse isn't allowed to help. He lives on the veranda (which is why you can't see him in the picture). 'Why on earth do you keep your horse on the veranda?' asks Tommy. All the horses he knows live in stables.

'Well,' says Pippi, 'in the kitchen he'd just be in the way. And he doesn't feel comfortable in the living room.' After a while, Tommy and Annika go home. But they are very happy to have a new friend.

i can braid her hair and button
her undershirt at the same time.

Not many people can do that.

When she washes herself, she dips
her whole head in the washbasin.
She likes to get water in her eyes.

Here she is eating. She lies on the table and puts her food on the chair. There's nobody to tell her to sit properly.

Once in a while, she'll scrub the
kitchen floor. She straps brushes on
her feet and pours a whole bucket of
water onto the floor. Then she skates
on the brushes.

When she chops wood, she never splits
fewer than five pieces at a time.

YUCK, the stove is full of smoke. Pippi has to go up on the roof and clean the chimney. She does everything herself.

'I'm a thing-finder,' says Pippi one day to Tommy and Annika.

'A thing-finder, what's that?' asks
Tommy.

'A person who finds things,' says
Pippi. 'The whole world is full of
things, and someone needs to find
them. And that's what a thing-finder
does.'

Tommy and Annika decide to
become thing-finders as well. Then
they all go out searching for things.

Pippi finds a rusty metal can.

'You can never have too many cans,' she says with satisfaction.

'What can you use it for?' wonders Tommy.

'You can stick your head in it and pretend it's the middle of the night,' says Pippi.

And she does. She walks along with the can over her head until she trips over a fence. What a racket!

CRASH!

But Pippi finds something else. An empty cotton reel.

'Such a sweet, sweet little cotton
reel to blow bubbles with or to hang
around your neck on a string,' she says
happily.

Tommy and Annika haven't found
anything.

'Why don't you look inside those tree stumps,' says Pippi. 'Tree stumps are among the best places for thing-finders.'

And guess what! Tommy finds a
nice notebook with a little silver pen.
And Annika finds a coral necklace.

Then the thing-finders go home–
Pippi with her can and cotton reel,
Tommy with his notebook, and
Annika with her necklace.

CHAPTER 3

Pippi at the Circus

The circus is in town.
Pippi buys tickets for
herself and Tommy and
Annika with one of her
many gold coins.

Pippi has never been to the
circus. She doesn't know how
it works.

She wants to perform, too.

Because Pippi can do anything.

The circus director gets mad.
The girl who was supposed to walk on
the high wire gets mad, too. But the
people at the
circus shout,

'GO, PIPPI!'

A pretty little circus girl comes riding in on a horse. She can stand up on her horse. But so can Pippi. She jumps up on the horse's back and stands behind the circus girl. The circus girl tries to push her off. She doesn't know how strong Pippi is.

'Why should you be the only one having fun,' says Pippi to the circus girl. 'I've paid, too.'

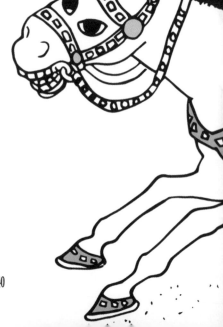

'**GO, PIPPI!**' scream Tommy and Annika and all the people at the circus.

Pippi knows even more tricks. The strongest man in the world is next. Strong Adolf is his name. The circus director promises a reward to the person who can wrestle Strong Adolf to the floor.

'I can,' says Pippi to Tommy and Annika.

'Even you can't do that,' says Annika.

'He's the **STRONGEST** man in the world.'

'And I am the **STRONGEST** girl,' says Pippi.

She goes right over to Strong Adolf and grabs him around the waist.

He's so surprised that his eyes almost
pop out of his head when he sees that
such a little girl wants to wrestle with
him.

But—one, two, three—Pippi throws
him up in the air and then she lays
him down on the floor.

'PIPPI'S WON, PIPPI'S WON!' scream the people at the circus.

CHAPTER 4

Pippi and the Robbers

When Pippi sleeps, she always puts her feet on the pillow and her head under the covers. That's how she likes to sleep, and there's no one to tell her not to. Mr Nilsson sleeps in a green doll's bed, but he doesn't put his feet on the pillow.

One dark night, two nasty robbers climb into Pippi's room. They want to steal the big bag with all the gold coins. They have no idea that Pippi is so strong.

'Ha, ha, we'll soon have the bag,' they say. And they snatch it.

But then Pippi shoots up out of bed.
In no time she's taken back the bag.

'We're not kidding,' says one robber.
'Give me that bag!' And he grabs
Pippi's arm hard.

'I'm not kidding, either,' says Pippi. She throws him up on top of a wardrobe.

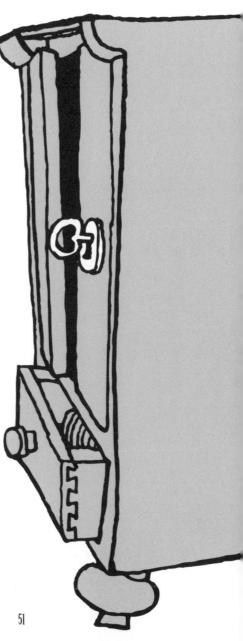

Then she throws the other robber up there, too. Both robbers are so scared they start to cry.

Pippi feels sorry for them and gives
them each a gold coin to buy food.
Because Pippi is kind. If you are very
strong, you must also be very kind.

CHAPTER 5

Pippi's Birthday

Soon it will be Pippi's birthday. And, of course, she is going to have a birthday party.

TMMY AN aNiKA ARE iNViTD TO PiPPi's BiRSDAY

She writes a letter to Tommy and Annika inviting them to the party. She doesn't write very well, because she hasn't gone to school like other children. But she does her best. Then she sneaks over and puts the letter in Tommy and Annika's mailbox.

Tommy and Annika are so happy when they find the letter. They can't wait to go to Pippi's party. They put on their nicest clothes and brush their hair.

And, of course, they buy a present for Pippi. They buy a music box and wrap it. They both hold the package when they go to Villa Villekulla.

When Pippi opens her present, she's so excited that she jumps up and down. She plays the music box for a long time. It has a pretty tune.

Pippi has set the kitchen table. She serves Tommy and Annika hot chocolate with whipped cream and lots of cookies and cake. She baked everything herself. Mr Nilsson is sitting on the table. Pippi's horse has also been invited to the party.

'I've never been to a birthday party with a horse before,' says Annika, and gives the horse a lump of sugar.

'Me, neither,' says Tommy. 'This is the best party I've ever been to.'

When Pippi has had her hot chocolate, she puts her cup upside down on her head like a hat. But it isn't completely empty. A little hot chocolate trickles down her face.

Afterward they play a game called *Don't Touch the Floor*. You play by climbing around the kitchen without ever touching the floor.

They jump from the sink to the stove and from the stove to the firewood chest and then they crawl across the shelf to the table and then up onto the cupboard in the corner and from the cupboard to the horse and from the horse back to the sink. It's a good thing the horse is there, so they can climb on him, too.

Pippi has a desk with many tiny drawers.

There are more magical things in that desk than in a whole toy store.

There are small dolls' dishes and trumpets, birds' eggs and unusual snail shells, knives with mother of pearl handles, and necklaces. In fact, there's too much to list it all.

Pippi wants to give Tommy and
Annika a present, even though it's not
their birthday. Tommy gets a little
ivory flute. Annika gets a brooch that
looks like a butterfly.

'That was the best party I've ever been to,' says Tommy.

'Yes, if only we could stay forever,' says Annika.

They wave to Pippi, and Pippi and
Mr Nilsson wave back.

Tommy and Annika have such a good time with Pippi they want to play with her every day.

HAVE ANOTHER ADVENTURE WITH PIPPI LONGSTOCKING!

What on earth is a snirkle? Is it something tasty to eat? Is it something you use to fight lions? Is it something that you need a doctor for? Pippi Longstocking can't believe it. She's made up a most excellent brand spanking new word: snirkle. The trouble is, she doesn't know what it means. There's only one thing for it. She's just going to have to go out and find one for herself.

TWO-COLOUR BLUE AND BLACK ILLUSTRATION

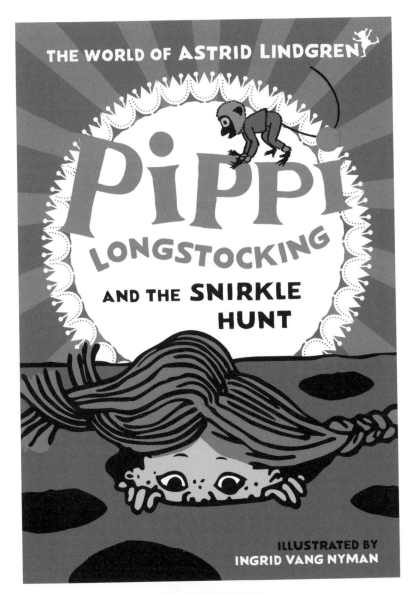

THE WORLD OF ASTRID LINDGREN

PiPPi
LONGSTOCKING
AND THE **SNIRKLE HUNT**

ILLUSTRATED BY
INGRID VANG NYMAN

978-0-19-277243-5

THE WORLD OF ASTRID LINDGREN

Want to read more about Pippi? Discover
the three classic Pippi books – packed with
extraordinary adventures and exploits, all in
Pippi's own unforgettable style!

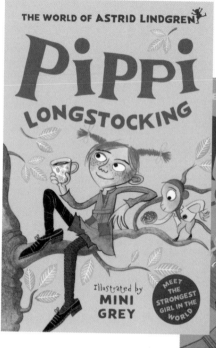

Now with stunning new
black and white illustrations
from Mini Grey.

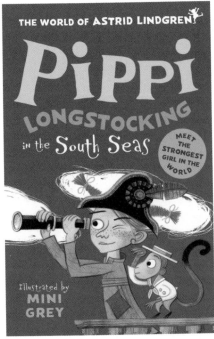

THE WORLD OF ASTRID LINDGREN

Meet Astrid Lindgren's other wonderful characters, and enter their world of freedom, fun, and outdoor adventures.

EMIL

The angelic-faced boy with a talent for trouble!

KARLSSON

When Karlsson flies into
Smidge's life, things will never
be dull again . . .

LOTTA

Small, stubborn,
and full of ideas. . .

THE CHILDREN OF
NOISY VILLAGE

Six children and a
world of free-range fun!

ABOUT THE AUTHOR

Astrid Lindgren was born in 1907, and grew up at a farm called Näs in the south of Sweden. Her first book was published in 1944, followed a year later by *Pippi Longstocking*. She wrote 34 chapter books and 41 picture books, that all together have sold 165 million copies worldwide. Her books have been translated into 107 different languages and according to UNESCO's annual list, she is the 18th most translated author in the world.

ABOUT THE ILLUSTRATOR

Ingrid Vang Nyman was born in 1916 in Vejen in southern Jylland, in Denmark. She took her work as an illustrator very seriously, worked very fast and had a high level of ambition. She demanded that illustrations for children should be of the same high artistic quality as for adults.

Ingrid Vang Nyman was *Pippi Longstocking*'s original illustrator and her classic artwork is recognized worldwide.

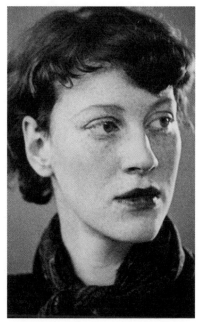